This book belongs to:

Heather♡
Dillon♡

A catalogue record for this book is available from the British Library

Published by Ladybird Books Ltd
80 Strand London WC2R 0RL
A Penguin Company

2 4 6 8 10 9 7 5 3 1

© Ladybird Books Ltd MMV

Endpaper map illustrations by Fred van Deelen

LADYBIRD and the device of a Ladybird are trademarks of Ladybird Books Ltd

ISBN-13: 978-1-84422-301-5
ISBN-10: 1-84422-301-9

Printed in China

LADYBIRD TALES

Goldilocks
and the
Three Bears

Retold by Vera Southgate M.A., B.Com

with illustrations by Yvonne Gilbert

Once upon a time there were three bears who lived in a little house in a wood.

Father Bear was a very big bear. Mother Bear was a medium-sized bear. Baby Bear was just a tiny, little bear.

One morning, Mother Bear cooked some porridge for breakfast. She put it into three bowls.

There was a very big bowl for Father Bear, a medium-sized bowl for Mother Bear and a tiny, little bowl for Baby Bear.

The porridge was rather hot so the three bears decided to go for a walk in the wood while it cooled.

Now at the edge of the wood, in another little house, there lived a little girl. Her golden hair was so long that she could sit on it. She was called Goldilocks.

On that very same morning, before breakfast, Goldilocks also went for a walk in the wood.

Soon Goldilocks came to the little house where the three bears lived. The door was open and she peeped inside. When she saw that no one was there, she walked straight in.

Goldilocks saw the three bowls of porridge and the three spoons on the table. The porridge smelled good and Goldilocks was hungry because she had not had her breakfast.

Goldilocks picked up the very big spoon and tasted the porridge in the very big bowl. It was too hot!

Then she picked up the
medium-sized spoon and tasted
the porridge in the medium-sized
bowl. It was too lumpy!

Then she picked up the tiny,
little spoon and tasted the
porridge in the tiny, little bowl.
It was just right.

Soon she had eaten it all up!

Then Goldilocks saw three chairs: a very big chair, a medium-sized chair and a tiny, little chair.

She sat in the very big chair. It was too high!

She sat in the medium-sized chair. It was too hard!

Then she sat in the tiny, little chair. It was just right!

But was the tiny, little chair just right? No! Goldilocks was rather too heavy for it. The seat began to crack and then it broke.

Oh dear! Goldilocks had broken the tiny, little chair and she was very sorry.

Next, Goldilocks went into
the bedroom. There she saw
three beds: a very big bed,
a medium-sized bed and a tiny,
little bed.

She felt tired and thought she
would like to sleep.

So Goldilocks climbed up
onto the very big bed. It was
too hard!

Then she climbed up onto the medium-sized bed. It was too soft!

Then Goldilocks lay down on the tiny, little bed. It was just right!

Soon she was fast asleep.

Before long the three bears came home for breakfast.

Father Bear looked at his very big porridge bowl and said in a very loud voice, "Who has been eating *my* porridge?"

Mother Bear looked at her medium-sized porridge bowl and said in a medium-sized voice, "Who has been eating *my* porridge?"

Baby Bear looked at his tiny, little porridge bowl and said in a tiny, little voice, "Who has been eating *my* porridge and has eaten it all up?"

Next, Father Bear looked at his very big chair. "Who has been sitting in *my* chair?" he asked in a very loud voice.

Then Mother Bear looked at her medium-sized chair. "Who has been sitting in *my* chair?" she asked in a medium-sized voice.

Then Baby Bear looked at his tiny, little chair. "Who has been sitting in *my* chair and has broken it?" he asked in a tiny, little voice.

Next, the three bears went into the bedroom. Father Bear looked at his very big bed. "Who has been lying on *my* bed?" he asked in a very loud voice.

Mother Bear looked at her medium-sized bed. "Who has been lying on *my* bed?" she asked in a medium-sized voice.

Baby Bear looked at his tiny, little bed.

"Here she is!" he cried, making his tiny, little voice as loud as he could. "Here is the naughty girl who has eaten *my* porridge and broken *my* chair! Here she is!"

At the sounds of their voices, Goldilocks woke up. When she saw the three bears she jumped off the bed in fright.

She rushed down the stairs, through the cottage door and disappeared into the wood.

By the time the three bears reached the door, Goldilocks was out of sight. The three bears never saw her again.